Amelia Bedelia Goes Back to School

by Herman Parish • pictures by Lynn Sweat

HarperFestival®

A Division of HarperCollinsPublishers

"Amelia Bedelia," said Maria,
"thanks for walking us to school."
"My pleasure," said Amelia Bedelia.
"Do you like school?"
"It's lots of fun," said Alex. "Can
you come spend the day with us?"

"May I stay?" asked Amelia Bedelia.
"Please do," said Miss Wilson, the teacher.
"You would be welcome."

"Good morning, class," said Miss Wilson.
"The bell has rung. Please take your seats."

"No, thank you," said Miss Wilson.
"Just sit down on it."
Amelia Bedelia put her seat
on the chair seat.

"Where should I take my seat?"
asked Amelia Bedelia.
"Should I take it out to the
playground?"

"All right, class," said Miss Wilson.
"I am going to give everyone problems."

Miss Wilson laughed, and said, "These hot dogs are different."

"They taste good," said Maria. "All these hot dogs need is mustard and ketchup."

"How nice,"
said Amelia Bedelia.

"What are they
serving the dogs?
Hot dogs need a
cool drink of water."

After lunch, it was time for art class.
"Paint anything you like," said Miss Wilson.

FARMER
TRACTOR
BARN

COW
CHICKEN
SHEEP

"You should stand back," said Miss Wilson.
"You will get chalk dust in your eyes."
"Thank you," said Amelia Bedelia.
"Now I can see the words."

FARMER
TRACTOR
BARN

COW
CHICKEN
SHEEP

"If you say so,"
said Amelia Bedelia.
She tried to put her eyes
on the chalkboard.

"Lunchtime," said Miss Wilson.
"Our cafeteria is serving hot dogs."

"It's okay," said Alex.
"We like math problems."
"Arithmetic is my favorite
subject," said Maria.

"No fair!" said Amelia Bedelia.
"The children have been
very good. You should not give
them any problems at all."

After arithmetic, the children erased the chalkboard.
"It's time for spelling," said Miss Wilson.
"Eyes on the board, please."

"Do not put paint on them,"
said Miss Wilson.
"Paint a picture *of* them."

"Good idea,"
said Amelia Bedelia.
"That will be less messy."

"I like Alex and Maria,"
said Amelia Bedelia.
"Hold still so I can paint
both of you."

After art class, it was time for reading.
"Let's read in a circle," said Miss Wilson.

"Please sit down," said Miss Wilson.
"You can join our reading circle."

Amelia Bedelia loved the story
they read.

"Read in a circle?"
asked Amelia Bedelia.
"Uh-oh, I am getting dizzy."

BRRRR-IINNNNG!

"School is over," said Miss Wilson.
"Will you come back tomorrow?"
"I do not think so," said Amelia Bedelia.
"Mrs. Rogers needs me and I need to rest."

"Me, too," said Miss Wilson.